Blossom

Laura Dockrill

Illustrated by
Sara Ogilvie

Barrington Stoke

First published in 2021 in Great Britain by
Barrington Stoke Ltd
18 Walker Street, Edinburgh, EH3 7LP

www.barringtonstoke.co.uk

A CIP catalogue record for this book is available
from the British Library upon request

ISBN: 978-1-80090-023-3

Printed by Hussar Books, Poland

For Tutu

Chapter 1

Did you know that plants are wonderful listeners? And they are *great* at keeping secrets too.

My grandma, Tutu, used to say, "You're never alone if you have a plant."

Thanks to Tutu, we have plants all over the house, so we are *never ever* alone. In fact, we are kind of overcrowded – and a bit outnumbered too. It's like the plants don't live with us, *we* live with the plants.

There is a group of plants gossiping by the front door, and the waxy palms by the TV mean we always have to watch TV shows at an angle.

Plants are draped like towels over the banister, twisting around the handrail and creeping up the walls like natural wallpaper.

We have plants in the bath, sticking their arms and legs out at you as they soak in the tub like they're on holiday! We have to use the shower – which would be fine but there are even a few plants in there too, crowded together like they are having a private dinner party! Honestly, the plants are EVERYWHERE! You can't even do a wee in peace!

There are plants on all the kitchen surfaces. Herbs that we use for cooking – chives, sage, basil, coriander, parsley – and ones that smell beautiful like lavender on the windowsill. Bees sometimes hover above them as if they're browsing in a supermarket!

Spider plants hang out on the fridge, sticking a nosy arm into whatever you're eating. And you are *sure* to get a sharp poke in the eye from something green when you do the washing-up. All these plants are trying to get your attention and to listen in on your thoughts.

Climbing the stairs are potted plants. They greet you as you go up to bed like the heads of seals: *bob, bob, bob.*

I always feel like they're *tee-heeing* when I get sent to my room for *talking back.*

You're probably thinking: why on earth would you let all of these plants take over your home?

And so I'll tell you – but it is a bit sad, so prepare yourself.

Chapter 2

My dad's parents, Tutu and Pops, lived in the most higgledy-piggledy house. If you think our house is covered in plants, you should have seen theirs! Some rooms looked like a jungle and their garden was wild and overgrown with fruit trees, roses, buds and bulbs!

Inside, ivy hung from the ceiling, and crept and crawled its way down the walls and around the banister! The kitchen had ACTUAL grapes dangling from vines above that you could just pick whenever you wanted a snack. My pops would lift me up and let me snap off a shiny fruit from its branches.

Tutu and Pops always chattered away to the plants. They said it helped them to grow. They told me, "Plants need a bit of company from time to time – just like us!"

I once asked Tutu what makes plants such good friends. She said, "You can learn a lot about friendship from a plant. Plants are wise

6

old advisors – they listen but allow you to find the answer on your own. They never judge us but are always there, helping to clean the air that we breathe and making us feel calmer. And plants don't ask for much in return – just some food, water and a bit of sunlight."

When I remember Tutu's words, I can't help but think about *all* the things I ask for. It's a *lot* more than that.

My tutu was just like a plant in lots of ways. The way I could tell her all my worries and she would just listen. The way she always knew how to keep me calm. But, unfortunately, Tutu and Pops aren't around any more. Tutu got sick and died, then Pops died shortly after. It all happened not long ago, just after I turned ten, and I'm still ten now. Everybody says Pops died of a broken heart and I believe that – Tutu was Pops's sunshine. And people, like plants, need sunshine.

My mum and dad had to sell Tutu and Pops's house and they donated all their furniture to the big charity shop. But Dad said it would make Tutu so upset if he gave all the plants away. Some of them were like family to Dad and had been around since he was a small boy.

There was a *letter*, too, from Tutu to my dad. It was written in her scribbly handwriting and told him to TAKE GOOD CARE OF OUR PLANTS! So there was no way he could let her down about that.

I remember Mum watching as the plants moved in to our already cramped house, one by one.

Dad would say, "Just one more." Then he'd drop off another van-load of plants, saying, "I can't get rid of this one – this one was Tutu's *special* one."

It seemed that nearly all the plants were Tutu's "special one".

Mum crossed her arms and shook her head at Dad as our small house was overtaken.

Chapter 3

But there's only one plant in my room.

It's an aloe vera and it is the greatest plant in the world.

Its leaves contain this gel that has magic properties. It can be used for medicine, to treat sunburn and even as mouthwash. But the best thing about my aloe vera is that she is my friend. Her one job is simply just to live with me.

She is green, but all different shades. Peppermint green in places, bottle green in others and apple green too. My plant has spiky edges a bit like a bread knife. Her leaves are sharp. Fleshy. Flecked. Speckled – like an egg. And she's *beautiful*.

She's small, not much bigger than a mug of tea, yet she's old – *way* older than me. She's even older than Mum and Dad and all of our ages added up together! She's tough and she's *very* proud of herself.

And she was Tutu's favourite plant of all. That is why she is so special to me.

When Tutu died, it was up to me to take care of the aloe vera. And so I think of her as Tutu Plant.

"Haloe, Vera," I say to her every morning. It's an in-joke between Tutu Plant and me.

You wouldn't get it.

Well, you probably would – it's just "hello" said like *aloe* with an *h* at the front.

I chatter away to Tutu Plant just like I would chatter to my grandma. It's made missing Tutu not so hard.

I talk to her all the time – when I'm worried, or scared, or confused, or angry ... or when I can't sleep at night. Tutu Plant is always there to listen to me.

I seem to be talking to her more than ever at the moment. And that's because things have been going wrong since my grandparents died.

Before bed, I can hear my parents arguing downstairs. I know what it's about.

You see, Tutu and Pops owned the most beautiful stall at a flower market. This is not a flower stall like the ones you see on high streets or at train stations where you can buy a bunch of flowers. No, this is where the magic *really* begins.

After flowers are picked from the ground, they are taken to a big market and then flower shops buy from the stalls at the market! Tutu and Pops's stall meant they worked at the roots of flower selling – helping bunches of flowers and plants find their way into our homes. After they died, the market stall became our responsibility. It is a BIG DEAL for us!

My dad is proud to carry on his parents' stall, running it the same exact way as Tutu and Pops did. I am going to join him as soon as I can – I just need to get this whole growing-up thing out of the way first. In the meantime, my mum has been helping Dad, and it isn't working out very well.

Having to help Dad look after the stall has come at the worst time for my mum. Before Tutu and Pops died, Mum gave up her job in a cafe to go back to college. She's studying chemistry (which is a fancy word for science) and another thing as well – I can't remember the name of it because it's such a difficult word. It's all very complicated but it's *very* impressive and if all goes to plan Mum could go on to do *amazing* things.

But now Mum says she has no space to study any more with the plants taking up all the room in our flat, and no time for studying on top of looking after the market stall. She says she's falling behind with her course and that Dad isn't supporting her. This was supposed to be "her time" to follow her dreams, Mum says. I can't imagine it being somebody's *dream* to go back to school like Mum has, but adults can be weird like that.

From my bedroom, I hear Mum downstairs calling the plants "stupid".

This is hurtful.

Dad says, "Well, what do you want then?"

And Mum says, "I don't know but not *this*."

I know what *this* means. It means *us*.

And not wanting *us* means that Mum and Dad don't love each other any more.

My parents lower their voices. I know it's so I can't hear what they are saying. But it's too late. I've already heard them.

Before bed, I take a big mouthful of water from my glass, filling my cheeks like a hamster. Then I shower the water out, sending a spritz all over Tutu Plant's leaves. She seems to shudder with thanks.

I switch off my nightlight and am plunged into darkness.

But I am not alone.

"Goodnight, Tutu," I whisper to Tutu Plant as she sits on my desk.

"Goodnight, Blossom," I almost hear her whisper back.

Chapter 4

The next morning, I am lying in bed. The first thing I hear is Dad's slippers going *brush*, *brush*, *brush* towards the bathroom.

I'm in the moment between asleep and awake, between real life and a dream.

"Haloe, Vera," I say to Tutu Plant.

I hear the door to the bathroom clicking open, followed by the squeaking sound of the tap … the pipes rattling … the toilet flushing. It's *that* time already!

"Hi, Dad," I whisper in the darkness.

My door creaks open and a mountain appears at the foot of my bed in the shape of Dad.

"Rise and shine, Blossom," he says. "If you're going to run the market stall one day, you have to learn to get up with the birds!"

"I am!" I say. "Look. I'm wide awake!"

I use my fingers to stretch my eyes open wide to prove it.

Dad laughs softly and mumbles, "OK."

Of course I'm awake. I've been going to the market *every* morning *every* day *all* summer during the holidays. Now my body knows exactly when I have to wake up. I'm like a dog. You know how dogs know the time without even understanding numbers? They just *know* when it's time to eat or go for a walk. Dogs just feel it in their bones. That's what I'm like now too.

I hear Mum groan awake. Poor Mum.
She stays up to study every night after Dad
and I have gone to bed – doing coursework
on her computer or bent over her textbooks
like a willow tree. She drinks coffee and eats
jelly babies to keep her awake.

Sometimes Mum doesn't even make it to bed. Dad and I come down in the morning and find her asleep at her desk or lying on the sofa under a pile of open books, their pages apart like the wings of a bird.

"It's just for a couple of weeks," Dad said when Mum agreed to help look after the market stall. But I think it's been a lot more work than Dad realised, and the weeks have turned into months ...

Chapter 5

It's much colder today and I have to peel my pyjamas off and quickly dress into my new clothes ALL under the covers. I don't want the stingy air to touch my skin yet. Outside it's dark. More than grey. The air is thick and scratchy like an itchy blanket.

"Summer is almost over," Tutu Plant sighs in a voice that only I can hear. "I love the change of the seasons," she adds, as if I needed reminding that it's chilly and I'm cold.

"That means the holidays are almost over too," I say. "Soon it will be time to go back to school. And you'll miss me then, won't you?" I add cheekily.

I can hear Mum and Dad crashing about downstairs now.

Mum's shouting something about the keys to the van.

Dad's shouting something about where he last saw them.

Mum's snapping back at Dad, calling the market "annoying".

"They're arguing again," I mutter to Tutu Plant.

"Be kind and gentle with your parents, Blossom," I hear her reply. "You don't know what they're having to cope with. Adults have lots of worries – remember that."

"I have worries too!" I point out.

"Yes, but do you have any *responsibilities*?"

Hmm ... other than brushing my teeth, not really. It makes me stop and take a breath.

Tutu Plant is right.

I wish Tutu was still alive.

I look fondly at the plant. The closest thing I have to my grandma.

Once I'm dressed, I make my way downstairs with Tutu Plant, as she always comes to work with us. She's so small and sturdy it's no problem.

The plants in the hallway roll their eyes as I leave my room. They're jealous of the special treatment I give Tutu Plant but I don't care.

"Get over it!" I tut.

"BLOSSOM!" Mum calls up.

"COMMMMMIIINNNNG!" I shout down.

The house smells of shampoo. Coffee. Toothpaste. *Home.*

No one on our street is awake – except the birds and the scruffy city foxes. And the woman opposite who does night shifts at the hospital, but that doesn't even count because she's going to bed now, whereas we are just getting started.

We pile into the van. I'm sandwiched in the middle. Squished in like strawberry jam as always, with Tutu Plant on my lap safe and sound.

The engine wakes with a groan. Mum drives along the empty roads, with honey light pouring from the streetlamps, guiding the early risers.

Builders appear in the warm spotlights, strolling towards the new apartment development in their hi-vis jackets. Their heads are down as they gaze at the bright squares of their silent phones. Cyclists weave between the traffic, soaring along lanes, slicing the air like scissors through wrapping paper.

The city is waking up.

And safe in the warm van, I can almost forget the arguments as we head to my favourite place in the world, me holding tightly onto Tutu Plant. I can almost forget that my parents don't seem to love each other any more. And I can almost trick myself into thinking that I might be the luckiest kid on this earth.

Chapter 6

We drive under the huge bright white sign
that says:

PEACHAM GARDEN FLOWER MARKET

It hangs in the charcoal sky like a GINORMOUS
toothy smile.

A massive orange peach dangles next to
the sign. Sometimes I imagine sitting inside
that peach, looking down at the cars in its
amber light.

We are here. The flower market.

We say hello to Richard at the gate.

"Morning, Blossom," he says from his Portakabin. It looks like a tiny sitting room trapped inside a phone box. Richard has made it cute, with a kettle, biscuits and a radio. Everything anybody needs.

"Morning, Richard," we reply.

"Cold today," Richard says. "The season's turning!" Soon Richard's Portakabin will be red and orange, a sauna of electric heaters.

"It'll soon be back to school for this one," Dad adds, nudging me in the ribs like the ULTIMATE embarrassing dad.

Annoying. Why did Dad have to bring up school? Talk about killing the mood.

"Oh no, we'll miss you here!" Richard says. "This is your *real* school, right, Blossom?"

I feel myself light up. *Yeah, Dad, this is my real school*, I think. *Soon I'll be the boss of our stall and then I can come here as much as I want!*

Richard waves us off, chuckling. "Have a good day, Blossom …"

"I will!" I say, because it's true. I will have a good day. I always have a good day at the flower market. Why would Mum *not* want to work here for ever? I don't get it.

Our van bounces happily between the bollards, chugging its way to the loading bay, where all the vans park up.

The weather *is* changing but I don't mind that when I am at the market. Autumn will come and then the trees will start shedding their leaves, stripping down to bare branches that look like frozen bear claws. It's weird – you'd think the trees would keep hold of their covering in the winter, not lose it!

The ground will be awash with the leaves, like mosaic floor tiles, red and orange, amber and brown. And crunchy like fish batter – fun to rush into and roll around in the park. There will be shiny conkers, pine cones and frost.

And here in the market we'll say goodbye to the sunflowers, freesias and lilies. We'll welcome in the roses, the orange snaps, berries, butterfly carnations, sweet williams, pods and shoots.

"Funny how you love changes in nature ..." Tutu Plant starts to say, babbling away from my lap.

"But I don't like change in my life?" I reply. "Yes, thank you, Tutu Plant." She's right again as always.

Once when I was younger, Tutu stopped me as we were walking down the street and pointed at a flower bursting out from a crack in the pavement. "Look at this flower," Tutu said. "It's finding a way to live despite being surrounded by concrete. Just like nature, we can learn to adapt too. Change can be difficult but we can always find a way to grow. Life might not be the same as it was, or even how we like it, but it's always OK in the end."

But change still scares me, like how secondary school scares me, like how Mum and Dad fighting scares me. Like how the future scares me. And sometimes things don't turn out *OK in the end.* Losing Tutu wasn't OK in the end. Not ever. Not one bit.

Chapter 7

The Peacham Garden Flower Market is an indoor market with bright white light bulbs that force you to wake up. There is nowhere to hide from the dazzling light.

And then the smell of flowers hits you. Mild and rich all at once. Fresh. Zesty. Energetic. Exotic. Popping. Hazy. Dreamy. Romantic. Minty. Of apples. Of berries. Of mushrooms. Musty. Perfumed. Woody.

It always feels thrilling to arrive in the market – like Christmas morning. We never know what is going to happen – what flowers and plants our customers will need or what special events they will need them for. That's what makes this job so exciting.

Our stall stands in the very same spot it has been in for nearly fifty years! Can you believe it? Fifty years of love. When he was my age

my dad would sit on the stall, just like I do now, with *his* parents – Tutu and Pops. He'd watch the flowers come in and out, the customers come and go.

We are a classic family stall. And lots of people come to us hoping for the famous *Pops and Tutu* experience that they always gave. Their personalities, their *way*. Their eye for something special.

I can still see Tutu and Pops now: the way Pops would yak on with some story about a particular plant or flower as if he was wasting a customer's time. But then, as if by magic, he would produce the most stunning selection of flowers that he knew would work perfectly for their special event. The customer wouldn't even have noticed Pops pulling *those* flowers from *there* or matching *this* with *that* with ease.

And I remember the way Tutu would gently talk to customers about their lives, helping them to sweep their problems into tiny workable piles whilst giving them words of wisdom. Then, BAM! There would appear the most amazing assortment of new plants Tutu had pulled from behind the counter, hand-picked and waiting patiently to be taken to the customer's shop.

So it's really up to us to make sure we run it exactly as Tutu and Pops did.

"The plants come first," my pops always reminded us. "If they aren't happy, nobody is."

I watch my mum and dad get the stall ready for the day. The plants look great but what about my parents?

I place Tutu Plant on the counter, next to the photo of Tutu and Pops, so she can watch on, ruling over her kingdom like a queen on her throne. Then I head over to Gabby's van to get my hot drink while Mum and Dad set up.

"Do you guys want anything?" I ask before I leave.

To which they always say no.

Gabby makes me the sweetest milk with the smallest pinch of coffee granules, all stirred up and frothy and served in a paper cup with chocolate powder sprinkled on top. Then she does me a round of toast on the softest, soggiest plain white bread with heaps of salty butter and smooth peanut butter on top of that. Cut into triangles on a round paper plate.

I offer to pay but she says, "Put your money away, Blossom. This one's on me." But I've never had to pay for a single *one*! In fact I'm pretty sure I've offered Gabby the exact same coin every day this summer and she has never taken it from me.

I have to be careful to eat my edible treasure from Gabby out of sight of Mum and Dad. I've learned from experience that they might have said they didn't want anything but once they see me with my warm and delicious pudding toast they'll *always* want a bite.

And have you seen my mum's bites? It's like trying to share toast with a shark! And then I'm left with the petals of Mum's teeth marks in my breakfast.

I balance my toast on my hand while being so careful not to spill my hot drink and shuffle away to find a peaceful spot.

I go past Mercy and her amazing flower furniture – *yes, she makes actual furniture from flowers*! Tables and chairs and even lamps and books!

Past George and his dog, Radish – their stall is a renovated caravan filled with potted plants and bulbs. They're always playing records from the 1960s and '70s.

Then there's Didi and her orchids. Didi looks like an actual orchid herself, with her towering hair and bright clothes.

And Gita and Nadiyah, who hand-make huge sweeping canopies of flowers to hang on ceilings and rooftops for special events.

Mossboy works with – you guessed it – moss. He makes scary monsters, weird spooky creatures and superheroes for film sets and private parties. His whole stall has dry ice up to your knees, like you're wading in an *actual real-life* swamp (even though I've never seen a swamp in real life).

It's all so exciting. I greet everyone as I pass:

Hi, everybody! Hello! Hiya! Good morning! Hi!

There's snoopy old Gilda. She's a wrinkly old lady in a long green coat who spends her whole entire day, *every* day, roaming around the stalls being nosy. Gilda always has her hands clasped behind her back like a teacher, stopping *here*

and *there* to smell *this* and sniff *that* and chat to whoever will listen about whatever flower or plant happens to take her interest.

Dad says not to talk to snoopy old Gilda because she's a "time waster" and never buys anything; she only "snoops" – which is another word for being nosy. But if you watch her closely, you'll see how much she helps out. It's the little things – she'll pick up loose leaves and thorns from the floor. She'll clear up litter to keep the market looking smart and put empty coffee cups from Gabby's van in the bin. Gilda sometimes even "borrows" a broom and has a sweep. She waters plants that look thirsty. For no other reason than *because*. And she never asks for a thank you.

I sneak around the back of the cacti stall run by Rain to eat my breakfast in peace. It's normally comforting to sit here because I'm close enough to hear Mum and Dad talking about the day ahead – while keeping my breakfast safe. But today is not like other days.

Today is when I hear something I can't unhear.

Chapter 8

"I can't do this any more," I overhear Mum say as I bite into my toast. Her voice is breaking and trembling. "You have to choose – me or the stall."

"That's not fair!" Dad says. "Don't make me choose." His voice is rasping and in whispers – he is angry but I can tell he is sad too. It's the same voice Dad used with the doctors at the hospital when they said there was nothing more they could do for Tutu.

"You're choosing the stall over me and my happiness," Mum cries. "This isn't what I want – this isn't what I chose."

"But I need help," Dad says. "There's too much to do here for just one person. We could have a good life running the stall together, like my mum and dad. Why can't you just be happy here?"

"Because I'm not happy," Mum replies, "I'm exhausted. This is your dream not mine, and you're asking me to put my life on hold. I've worked too hard to give it all up now. Pretending to be happy here would be a lie. A lie to myself, a lie to you and a lie to Blossom."

Mum takes a breath, clears her throat, and in the same voice she uses to tell me off she says, "I can't go on like this. You have to sell the stall or ..."

"Or ...?" Dad says.

Before I know it, I am standing there. Standing right in front of them with a look on my face that lets Mum and Dad know I've heard everything.

"Or what?" I ask.

But the answer is as glaring as the sharp, harsh market lights. It is screaming me in the face.

How could I not see it until now? How could I not tell? All the fighting. All the arguments. All the huffing and puffing and slamming.

Mum on one side.

Dad on the other.

Mum has tears coming down her face.

Dad has worry and tension weighing him down like a goblin rucksack.

They are breaking up, aren't they? My parents are going to break up.

But the plants are happy, I tell myself. I look at Tutu Plant, at all the others on the stall – they are happy, so how come we're not?

I feel fear rise in me, and it makes my cheeks go horribly hot. A lump forms in my throat so big it feels like it's full of dry soil.

Mum and Dad look at me, frowning with shame. Dad says, "Blossom—"

But I interrupt, "No." It comes out as a tiny pathetic whimper. "Please don't ..." I suck my tears back, a burning feeling roaring up inside me. "Please don't break up."

I look to Tutu Plant for an answer but she's silent. She's out of ideas on this one. She looks on with sorrow.

"Please," I plead with Mum. "Please just think some more."

Mum sighs. "Blossom, my flower, all I do is think! I can't run the stall with your dad and have time to study. It's just too much of a stretch."

Dad looks annoyed at Mum. "It's not just about the time," he says. "It's your mum – she doesn't want to keep the stall."

Oh. I glare at Mum with disappointment and rage. *How could she do this to us? To Dad? To Pops and Tutu? TO ME? I was going to take over this place one day! We can't lose it!*

Mum looks back at Dad in shock – I can tell she's hurt that I'm hurt.

"You're so selfish!" I scream at Mum. "You only think about yourself!"

"That's not true, Blossom," Mum argues back. "You don't know the full story! It's not as simple as that!"

"You're telling Dad he has to SELL Tutu and Pops's stall or you're going to LEAVE him!" I shout. "Sounds pretty simple to me." I snatch Tutu Plant from the counter.

"Blossom, please, if I can just explain—"
Mum says, but I'm already walking off. My
sadness has turned into anger.

"I love you—" Mum starts to say.

"Well, I *hate* you!" I roar back. The words
come out of me like shards of glass that are
cutting my tongue. I know they are bad words
to say but I don't care – and so I begin to run ...

Chapter 9

I run and run and run. My heart is beating out of my chest. I have Tutu Plant under my arm to keep her safe as I pound towards the outside world.

I have no plan. I have no idea where I'm running to. I'm just running. From my parents. From the changes that are going to happen whatever I say or do.

I am scared. And I begin to cry. And then I am crying and running.

Crunning.

Oh, great.

I'm crunning to the sound of Mum shouting, "BLOSSOM!" and Dad shouting, "BLOSSOM!" and Mum explaining, "It's not your fault ..." and, "It doesn't mean that ..." and, "If you could just listen ..." and, "One day you'll understand ..."

I crun past George's records singing out and Radish starts barking. She senses the change. Knows something is wrong.

Rain is jumping up after me.

Mercy is shouting, "Why are you running, baby? What's going on?"

Flower stems roll off Gita's lap as she leaps up to follow me.

Didi is frozen, her face twisted.

Gabby stops in the middle of serving a customer, steam streaming from the coffee machine. I push past the people, the plants, the flowers, the air.

Why am I running from my happy place? From the family where I belong? The market? The faces I love that keep me safe?

What will happen if I lose my parents, my home AND the market all at once? Where will I go?

I'm scared.

I can't breathe. I spin, navigating my way between the maze of buckets and barrels, bumping into baskets and bins. Every flower has a head and a face and a nosy pair of eyes.

GO AWAY! GO AWAY! GO AWAY! I tell them.

I stagger into Mossboy's stall – a swampy garden, lit like a film set for a horror movie about some river monster. It has green and purple moonlight effects and a smog of dry ice.

I've lost my bearings.

I can't see.

My head feels like a washing machine.

Out of nowhere a moss monster
appears before me, its face fixed in a scare:
RAAAAAAAAHHHHHHHH!

I stumble backwards into the arms of
another moss monster with a screaming muddy
mouth. There's damp earth behind me, soil in
my hair.

I yelp.

Pant.

Leap up.

My heart in my throat.

Belly upside down.

I knock over more pots and plants.

"Sorry, sorry, sorry," I say. "Um ... I ...
excuse me ... sorry ..."

"Blossom, are you OK?" Mossboy asks, but his
voice sounds like a drill and then fades away.

I jump up. *Where is Tutu Plant?*

She's rolled away, skidding ahead. I jump up
to get her, scoop her up under my arm and keep
running. By now the market is alive with my
commotion. Everybody seems to be watching
me or shouting my name. Yet I've never felt
more lost.

Just keep running and it might stop, I
tell myself. *Just keep running and it might
change ... this time for the better.*

I spot Gilda being nosy, staring at me. *Oh,
not you, Snoopy Gilda, GO AWAY!*

And then I stumble into a wall of garden tools.

CRASH!

I trip over a small metal trowel – *OUCH* – and Tutu once again goes flyyyiiiinngg across the market and then …

CRACK!

Tutu Plant's pot is smashed into pieces, lying in chalky rubble on the ground. There's soil everywhere, splattered like blood. She's come loose from her pot and is sprawled in the middle of the market like an injured bird. The delicate tangle of her roots on display, her veins.

"Oh no! Tutu Plant!" I say, and rush towards her. A surge of pain floods through me. I feel a prickly hotness spiking into my whole body like a million needles. When I look up, I see a flash of a familiar green coat. Snoopy old Gilda

is there on her hands and knees beside me,
picking up the broken pieces of Tutu Plant's pot.

"Never mind," Gilda says, stuffing Tutu
Plant's soil into her hand. "Some people would
say it's a blessing when we break into pieces –
it gives us the chance to rebuild."

Snoopy old Gilda holds my hands and stands me up on my feet. I am in so much shock that I can't even find the words to reply as she dusts down my knees and says, "Now let's get you back to your mum."

Maybe Gilda isn't so bad after all?

Mum is already standing right by us with her arms open to pull me in, and Gilda has vanished as if she was never even there at all. I jump back but Mum holds me close. People are staring. I shoo her away, saying, "Mum, leave me alone, you're embarrassing me!"

"Blossom—" she begins to say.

I cry some more. "Why do you have to do this to us?" I ask. Snot is now running down my face. I bundle up broken Tutu Plant safely in my arms.

"Come here, my little one," Mum says. "I want to show you something." She lifts me up and carries me like a child over her shoulder. It's nice to feel small like a baby again, even if I am still mad with her, even if I feel like kicking and screaming.

I can't stay angry when Mum makes me feel so safe. I can smell her hair – woody and earthy. She takes me round to the loading bay where it's colder and less crowded. "OK …" Mum says, and gets her phone out. She begins scrolling.

Get on with it then, I'm thinking.

"Where's it gone now?" Mum mutters under her breath. "Hold on …" She's really killing the mood now. "It's here somewhere … ah, here it is."

"What is it?" I say.

Mum flips her phone around. "This was me," she says.

It's a photo of Mum around the same age as I am now. Our faces are almost identical except she has the cutest big gap in her top teeth. She is holding a big trophy decorated with ribbons.

"It was for a science project at school," Mum says, smiling fondly at the photo. "And this one here was when we went to my dad's exhibition at the Science Museum! Remember, my father was a scientist too!"

Mum as a little girl in the photo almost seems to come to life like a film. There she is, looking just like me – her happy dad proudly holding her up in his arms, soaring her to the moon. It's hard to imagine Granddad doing that now, as he's old and retired.

I feel bad. My mum has a story too. My mum has a history. My mum has dreams. And ambitions. I was thinking *she* was the selfish one, but really it depends what bit of the story you are looking at.

"I'm sorry, Mum," I say.

"I'm sorry too, Blossom," Mum says softly. "If we can't find somebody else to work at the market, we're going to have to sell the stall on."

And I know she is right. Mum's worked so hard to follow her dreams. She can't give it all up. But I wish there was a way we could make everybody happy.

I look once again at Tutu Plant. I'll start by fixing her. I can make a splint from a wooden ice-lolly stick and re-plant her in a temporary pot whilst I mend hers. She'll be all right ... and then it hits me.

An idea. A stroke of genius. A way to save the day!

I can run the stall with Dad.

I CAN RUN THE STALL WITH DAD!

Chapter 10

I walk back towards our stall with Mum. Dad is sitting with his head in his hands. He looks really tired and sad.

"Oh no! What happened to Tutu Plant?" is the first thing Dad asks.

"It's OK," I reply. "I'll fix her." I nod firmly and take a breath. "I've got something to say, Dad."

Mum looks surprised.

"OK?" Dad says.

"I'll run the stall with you, Dad," I announce.

"Huh?" Both my parents almost seem to laugh, and their frowns relax.

"*You?*" Dad asks.

"Yes, me!" I say. "I can tie bouquets. I can serve customers, I can tidy up, I can count money. I can do all the things you do. You need someone to help, so why can't it be me?"

"I don't think so, flower," Mum begins. "What about school?"

"What ABOUT school?" I argue back. "You have your dreams, Mum, and I have mine too! We all know I'm going to be running this place sooner or later, so why don't I just get started now?"

I begin working on the stall to show I am the perfect candidate for the job. I pull stalks from boxes, lift crates and arrange displays. *"See?"* I say.

"Blossom, we have no doubt you'd be fantastic working here, but you're still a kid," Dad points out.

"Please, just give me a shot," I say.

"I really don't think—"

"PLEEEEEEAAAAASSSSSEEEEE?"

Mum looks at Dad. Dad looks at Mum. The flowers look at me. I tie my apron around my waist a bit tighter, roll up my sleeves and get to work.

I fill the buckets with water from the squeaky copper tap and carry them back without spilling a drop, even though they're so heavy. I wrap flowers and talk to customers – Mr Shai about his wedding plans, Holly about her birthday, Lisa about the town hall's

ballroom-dance fundraiser and some clowns
about the circus that's coming to our local park.

I sweep leaves with the bristly broom that looks like it's from the Victorian days. I tidy displays and hang wreaths. I feed plants and spritz stalks. I count coins and add up receipts. And then I double-triple count everything to be certain. Plus my maths isn't *so* great.

At the end of the morning I am totally exhausted with that proud feeling you only get when you've worked really hard at something you care loads about. I collapse onto some empty cardboard boxes.

"So ... have I got the job?" I ask Dad.

"You did really well today, Blossom. In fact I think you ran the stall better than me ..." Dad sighs. "But I'm afraid you can't have the job yet, petal. You have to go back to school. We're sorry."

I tried. I really tried today. But clearly I need to come up with a new plan.

Chapter 11

It's a new day.

"Morning, Tutu," I say to Tutu Plant. I check to make sure her lolly stick is still wedged under her leaves. From my bed I see rain at the window. Thick hard droplets smatter and pound the glass like tears. *Great*. But I'm not going to let a miserable day stop me.

I drag myself out of bed with a rush of enthusiasm. If I'm not allowed to help Dad run the stall, then I'm going to find someone who can!

I wrestle with a mini orange tree at the kitchen table to get some space, then make some adverts asking for people to apply to work with Dad at the market. I use green crayon to decorate the sheets with plants and leaves. I loop big flowers in pink and in orange and write:

Are you looking for a job?
Some magical inspiration?
Would you like to make new friends?
Are you kind? Caring? Friendly?
Good with Nature?

Do you like plants and buttery toast
with the option of thick peanut butter?

If so, apply for a trial by simply
emailing my dad at ...

But before I can even write his email address Dad looks over my shoulder and says, "Oh no, Blossom," in a not-very-happy-voice, but then Mum glares at him from across the table.

"What a good idea, Blossom," Mum says, smiling in approval.

When we arrive at the market, I can't wait to wind down the window and tell Richard at the gate, "We're hiring!"

"Oh!" Richard sounds surprised. "You are?"

"YEP!" I beam, delighted with myself.

"Err ... *sort of*," Dad replies.

"We're just putting the feelers out," Mum says, almost correcting me.

"*Feelers?* What does that mean?" I ask.

"It means just ... you know, seeing if anybody is interested," Mum says. "Like scattering seeds ... but not *planting* anything."

Oh. Right.

"I suppose the job is only temporary," I explain to Richard. "You see, this is just until I finish school and then I'll be taking over Tutu and Pops's stall permanently for ever. So it will just be a job for someone for a few years."

"Right ..." Richard replies.

"Will you hang up one of the posters outside your cabin for us?" I ask.

"Of course," Richard says. He unrolls my advert and glitter tumbles down his front and onto the floor. "It's beautiful." He grins and his gold tooth twinkles.

"Thank you! Time to get those *feelers* out," I say. I've got a very good feeling about this.

Inside the market I hand posters around to all the stalls. Rain puts my poster up next to her cacti and George pins one to his notice board. Mercy tapes hers to her desk and Gita and Nadiyah take a photo of it to send to their friends. Even Didi puts the poster on display and she never normally puts anything up that isn't 100 per cent orchid-related! Mossboy says it's "wicked" and tells me that I'm a great artist.

"Thank you, Mossboy, but I don't want to be an artist," I tell him. "I want to run the stall like Tutu and Pops did."

"Your tutu and pops were both artists!" he replies, and he is absolutely right – they were.

I tell everybody that we are doing a trial for a brand-new position. Dad is following me around, telling people it's not a big deal, but I just ignore him. He can be so annoying.

The last poster goes up in Gabby's van, proudly displayed next to the prices for bacon butties and hot chocolates.

I am very confident we will find the right person.

Now all we have to do is wait.

Chapter 12

The responses to my adverts come flying in.
It's not surprising – Tutu and Pops's stall is very
famous and loved and respected. Dad says he's
never had so many emails!

We count up the applicants and find we have
twenty in total. There *must* be a suitable one in
there somewhere!

I FINALLY get Dad to agree to some
interviews. We have decided that IF a person
impresses us in the interview, then they can
have a trial shift with Dad. And IF they impress

us during their trial shift, then – and ONLY then (says Dad) – they will get the job.

Dad isn't *so sure* about the whole idea, but Mum says, "Why not? What's the worst that can happen?"

*

It turns out that quite a few *not so great* things can happen when you let strangers have a trial shift on your beloved stall …

TRIAL NO. 1 is Niko, who applied for the job because he likes to talk to plants. Perfect, we thought. He's just like Tutu and Pops, we thought. WRONG! What we did NOT expect was for Niko to pull up a chair and talk *at* the poor peonies about his love life and his terrible back pain for three hours. Mum has to give him a box of tissues and three sugary teas before he even thinks about leaving the trial/therapy session.

TRIAL NO. 2 is Elma Magori Stump – a woman who's like a giant angry T-rex. She storms up to the counter with fists like swinging bowling balls and begins to tell Dad how he's useless at running a flower stall. The tiniest thing makes her annoyed – like if Dad doesn't cut the sticky tape in a straight line – and after just a few minutes she has ripped her apron off and called Dad a "SALAD!" That is the last we see of her.

TRIAL NO. 3 does not even show up.

"I think Blossom's earned a bowl of chips and a lemonade!" Dad says kindly at the end of the week, but I feel so disappointed that not even chips and lemonade will cheer me up.

The trials were a disaster. Mum and Dad gave me a chance to find an employee for the stall and I've failed. I didn't realise it was going to be so hard.

And I know what's coming next – SCHOOL. Soon I'll be back there and Tutu and Pops's stall will be sold. My chances of ever becoming the proud owner and carrying on the family tradition will disappear like fallen blossom in the breeze.

Chapter 13

I don't sleep the night after the last trial – the one that didn't even get to happen. I watch the dark sky go from black to blue to pink to white. I go back to school tomorrow, so today is my last day at the market – probably ever.

Unless a miracle happens, Dad will have to start taking down the stall. The plants will all have to be sold. The money will be counted for the last time. The photo of Tutu and Pops will have to come down.

We all get ready and are silent – except for the purr of the kettle, the squeak of the bathroom tap, the hum of the van's engine. Nobody is happy, not even Mum. I can tell that she feels guilty for something I now realise isn't even her fault.

It's even more quiet than usual in our van as we spiral our way up the road and towards the loading bay. As we get to our stall we see Gilda snooping around in her long green coat.

"Oh, here we go," Dad grumbles. "The last thing we need!"

"Leave it, Dad. She's really nice," I reply, thinking of how Gilda helped me when I fell over.

"Morning, Gilda. How can we help you?" says Mum.

"I'm here for a trial," Gilda says.

Snoopy Gilda is here for a trial? I didn't even know she had applied!

"Sorry, Gilda," says Dad. "There's an interview process first before a trial." He thinks that will be the end of the conversation.

"Did you not get my application?" Gilda is confused.

"Errr ..." Dad starts, getting all flustered.

Dad mumbles something about his emails always getting lost and I realise that maybe *just* maybe Dad wasn't *completely* honest about all the applications he received. He must have decided not to tell us that Snoopy Gilda applied!

"We have decided to sell the stall now," Dad says, not looking Gilda in the eyes. "So, change of plan – thanks but no thanks, Gilda, we're no longer hiring."

Gilda looks disappointed. She has her cute little trainers on ready for a working day. "Ah, never mind," Gilda mutters, and turns to walk away.

Mum and I both turn and glare at Dad. We give him the look that Mum gives me when she can't tell me off with words in public places. Our eyes are like lasers cutting through him.

Dad sighs like a sulky teenager and reluctantly he says, "Gilda, hold on ..."

Chapter 14

Maybe Gilda picked up all her tricks during the long hours she's spent in Peacham – collecting leaves and sweeping and watching and watering. Maybe she discovered exactly what to do from silently wandering, buzzing from stall to stall like a summer bee with a constant content smile spread across her wrinkled face. Perhaps all that earwigging and spying gave Gilda the ability to handle flowers and plants with care and kindness. Because she just knows how to *be* with them.

In Gilda's trial, her gentle, strong, capable hands treat any root or stem or stalk or bud or

bulb with care and respect. Gilda is a natural.
Gilda was not a snooper – she was a wallflower.
And now she is ready to bloom.

At the end of Gilda's trial shift, Mum and I are ready for Dad to come up with any excuse about why it wouldn't work out with Gilda ... but he doesn't. Dad just waves goodbye to Gilda and says, "Same time tomorrow?"

We pile into the van in silence. Mum on one side, Dad on the other in the driver's seat and me squished in the middle. And then, out of nowhere, Dad begins to cry. I rush to hold his hand. His fingers feel rough, warm and familiar.

"What's the matter?" Mum asks Dad, wrapping an arm around him.

"It was the strangest feeling ..." Dad says softly, his eyes filled with tears. "It sounds stupid, but it felt like my mum was there beside me when I was running the stall with Gilda this morning."

Dad looks out into the world ahead and then at his worn hands gripping the car key. "It felt like I was there with your tutu," he says to me.

I hug him hard. Poor Dad.

"And how did that feel?" Mum asks him.

"Normal," says Dad. "It felt normal."

Chapter 15

I think back to when Tutu was in hospital.

Tutu was sitting up in bed, wearing a yellow nightdress with a blue cardigan. She was listening to the radio. Pops was by her side, holding her hand, which was blistered with age and swollen like a bruised plum. Both of their eyes were wet, but they were always wet those days, so I was used to it.

Tutu's face lit up when she saw me, her cheeks sagging with age but round and furry like the skin of a peach. Pops left with Mum to go and get a cup of tea.

Tutu and I talked for a bit. Then she reached to her side table and handed me Tutu Plant, who looked dignified and graceful in her smart little pot. "This is my special aloe vera plant," Tutu said gently, like I didn't already know. "I want you to take care of her for me."

"Why can't you take care of her yourself?" I asked, scared of the responsibility and of the answer too.

Tutu laughed to herself. "I'm not going to be around to be able to, Blossom. My final season is up."

"I'm scared," I said. Before I knew it, hot messy tears began to splash down my face and my heart was thumping out of my chest, beating against my ribcage. I didn't know where to put a feeling like that. "I'm scared of losing you."

"How can you lose something that is right *here*?" Tutu said. She held my face with one hand and put the other on my chest. My heart began to steady and calm down. "How can you lose someone when their roots are linked with yours, when they are a part of you? It is impossible."

I breathed her in and finally asked, "Where will you go?"

"Oh, you'll see ..." Tutu said. "Nowhere and everywhere."

And my tears blurred my eyes so much that the floor almost seemed awash with petals.

I see it now, like I never had before. As Mum and I were leaving, someone was knocking on the door to say hello, a face I recognised in a long green coat. I remember my tutu looking so happy to see her old friend. It was Gilda.

Of course it was – it was Gilda.

Chapter 16

I go back to school. I learn that I like other things as well as plants. I like learning about the planets and making a papier-mâché rocket with Anisha. And understanding how the wheel was invented. And cutting and sticking with Miles.

I like learning how to make a spider toy from wood with Remi and Tunde. Learning how many bones are in the human body and how penguin dads take care of the eggs. I learn that two digestive biscuits with melted marshmallow and chocolate can become something pretty special with Sam and Rukmini. And how magnets work with Tor. I suppose I also like making new friends – friends that are not just plants.

We manage to give some of our plants to loving homes (basically to all of our friends at the market!). Now our house feels less crowded. And Tutu Plant is all better and thriving. She still goes to the market every day to keep Gilda and Dad company – and bosses them about, I'm sure!

Mum passes all of her exams with distinction. After we get the news, we go for a big picnic in the park. We sit by a lavender bush, under a big tree.

Dad is so proud of Mum. And so am I. And so is the whole market. They throw a little party for her and we eat fruit cake from Gabby's van and raise our glasses to Mum.

And as a present to Mum we frame the photograph of her when she was a little girl being held up by her father into the sky.

Mum cries when we give the photo to her, and hugs each and every one of us.

Because to make a dream, it takes a team.

Just like it takes a tree to make blossom.